The Billy-Goats Tough

A play by Tim O'Brien

Illustrated by Robert Mancini

Collins

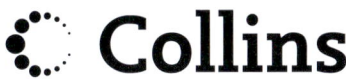

Characters

Narrator
(Storyteller)

Little Billy-Goat Tough
(L.B.G.T)

Super Billy-Goat Tough
(S.B.G.T.)

Borisina Dracula

Group of Four People

Brian Troll

Advertiser

Audience

Turn to pages **21**, **22** and **23** for Sound and Stage Tips

The Billy-Goats Tough

Scene 1

(Somewhere in the mountains. There is a little footbridge centre stage and a tree stump mid-stage right. The Narrator stands to the extreme left of stage. A hairy Troll, Brian, sits on the stump and looks grumpily at the Audience.)

Brian: G'day you creeps! I'm the Troll.

Audience: Boo! Hiss!

Brian: Ah, go and bite yourselves. I don't care if you don't like me. No one is meant to like me. I'm just hateful and nasty.

Narrator: As you well know, the Troll's job is to scare billy-goats that try to cross the bridge. Look, here comes Little Billy-Goat Tough now.

L.B.G.T: *(Enters from left stage, stops at the footbridge and waves at the Troll.)* Hello Mr Troll, can I cross your bridge?

Brian: What for?

L.B.G.T: I want to go to the pasture that's got all the yummy grass on the other side of the river.

Brian: All right, but it will cost you heaps. This is a toll troll bridge, you know.

L.B.G.T: How much does it cost?

Brian: *(Walking over to L.B.G.T.)* How much have you got?

L.B.G.T: *(Checking pockets for money.)* I've only got $3.75.

Brian: *(Snatching the money.)* Lucky for you that's exactly the right amount.

Audience: Boo! Hiss!

Narrator: So, Little Billy-Goat Tough clip-clopped across the bridge to the fresh, green pasture on the other side.

(Suddenly, a Group of People rushes on stage. They stop and begin pointing in all directions.)

Group: Look … up in the air … no … on the ground … near the bridge … is it a bird? … is it a sheep? It's … it's SUPER BILLY-GOAT TOUGH!

(They all rush off again as a Billy-Goat in tights, jocks and a cape leaps in from stage left.)

S.B.G.T: *(Leaping about and flexing muscles.)*
Ta-da! Get an eyeful of this bod. Oh, I'm so
terrific and wonderful, I scare myself. *(Stops to
make a speech.)* And I believe in truth … and
justice … and goodness and niceness …

Audience: *(Slapping foreheads.)* Good grief!

S.B.G.T: And I also believe in a good disguise …
(Puts glasses on.) … so that disguised as
mild-mannered Billy-Goat Tough,
I can fight for …

Brian: Stop it, I think I'm gonna throw up.
Who does he think he is, Wonder Woman?

S.B.G.T: Aha! A not-so-nice Troll!

Brian: Look, Fancy-Pants, would you just nick off?
There's always someone on my bridge, day in,
day out, clop-clop here, clop-clop there …
it's driving me bats!

Dracula: *(Rushing onto the stage.)* Bats? Bats you say? Did I hear you say bats?

Narrator: Go away, Dracula … you're not on until Scene 2 … see, it says so here in the script!

Dracula: What! No Dracula? No bats? Drats! *(Dracula swoops around snarling at the Audience and rushes out.)*

Brian: See, what did I tell you? There's always someone on the bridge!

S.B.G.T: Too bad, Troll. That's just your punishment for being nasty and bad. Stiff cheese, I say! Well, I'm off to find some goodness and niceness. *(S.B.G.T. bounces across the bridge.)*

Brian: Wait! *(To Audience.)* He didn't even pay the toll.

Narrator: So ends Scene 1: no toll for the Troll, no bats for Dracula, and a Billy-Goat who wears his underpants on the outside. It's all getting confusing. To give you time to catch your breath, let's take a short commercial break.

Advertiser: *(Rushing in from stage right, holding a brightly coloured bottle.)*

Hello everybody … now don't touch that dial … let me ask you something. Are you sick and tired of your hair? You put it up and it flops down, you comb it flat and it sticks straight up, your friends laugh at you and say 'Hey, who nailed that cocky to your head?' Well, friends, your problems are solved. With this tonic here … HAIR-EX … you'll never have a bad-hair-day again. Just rub this into your scalp, and we guarantee that all your hair problems will be solved. In fact, if you're not completely bald in four days, we will give you your money back.

So remember, get rid of all that unsightly hair with HAIR-EX!

(Advertiser rushes offstage. Brian fiddles uncomfortably with his hair.)

Audience: Boo! Hiss!

Scene 2

(Nothing has changed. Brian is sitting on his stump glaring at the Audience.)

Narrator: So we begin Scene 2. Will Super Billy-Goat Tough find some goodness and niceness? Will the Troll lose his bad temper somewhere and then grump and growl trying to find it? We will see … now enter Ms Borisina Dracula!

Audience: Hooray! We think.

Dracula: *(Leaping in from stage left.)* They seek me here, they seek me there, they seek this vampire everywhere! Nyuk, nyuk, nyuk, nyuk!

(Dracula starts to walk across the bridge. Brian stands and folds his arms.)

Brian: Just a minute, creepy one … now where do you think you're going?

Dracula: Nyuk, nyuk, nyuk … across the bridge, hairy. I'm on my way to the Blood Bank. It's time I made another withdrawal.

Brian: Well, you've got to PAY to cross MY bridge.

Dracula: Bats in garlic! Why?

Brian: It's in the story, creepy, that's why.

Dracula: A story! Nyuk, nyuk, how boring. I don't care about any silly old story.

Brian: Well, I didn't make it up. I hate the story. I can't stand my job. And I REALLY can't stand those …

S.B.G.T: *(Suddenly leaping in, cape flying.)* Aha! There you are! Dracula, hold it right there, you're under arrest. Your teeth marks are all over the Blood Bank.

Dracula: You'll never take me alive!

Audience: Naturally!

(There is a terrific fight: Dracula flits and swoops, S.B.G.T. leaps, rolls and high kicks. Finally, using a clever combination of judo, oregano and karate, S.B.G.T. overpowers Dracula.)

S.B.G.T: Aha, got you! Goodness wins again!
(To Audience.) I'm wonderful really, aren't I?
Actually, I'm so terrific I think I deserve
a prize.

(He begins posing and flexing his muscles and forgets about Dracula. Suddenly, Dracula and Brian grab him and give him the old heave-ho onto his bottom.)

Dracula and Brian: Take that, you super stomach ache!

Audience: Hooray!

S.B.G.T: Ouch! Ooh! That hurts … you're not fair …
Ooh! I'm gonna tell on you, just you wait!

(He dashes out holding his bottom.)

Dracula and Brian: *(Shaking hands.)* That's a job well done!

Dracula: Listen Troll, let me take you away from all this. We can hang around my castle and live scarily ever after.

Brian: Thanks creepy. Look, call me Brian.

Dracula: Brian … that's a good name for a Troll. You can call me Borisina.

Brian: *(Putting an arm on Dracula's shoulder as they walk off.)* Borisina, this could be the start of a beautiful friendship!

Audience: Good grief! How mushy!

Narrator: Well … that was a happy ending, wasn't it? Borisina and Brian got married and now they live in a nice little castle right next to Mr and Mrs Warlock and Bruce Werewolf. And do you know … every night, when the moon is full, they all have a lovely time scaring each other to death.
But that's another story for another time …

Sound and Stage Tips

About this play

This play is a story that you can read with your friends in a group or act out in front of an audience. Before you start reading, choose a part or parts you would like to read or act.

There are ten main parts in this play, plus the Audience, so make sure you have readers for all the parts.

Reading the play

It's a good idea to read the play through to yourself before you read it as part of a group. It is best to have your own book, as that will help you too. As you read the play through, think about each character and how they might look and sound. How are they behaving? What sort of voice might they have?

Rehearsing the play

Rehearse the play a few times before you perform it for others. In *The Billy-Goats Tough*, it is fun to act out the 'over-the-top' melodrama and slapstick humour.

Remember you are an actor as well as a reader. Your facial expressions and the way you move your body will really help the play to come alive!

Using your voice

Remember to speak out clearly and be careful not to read too quickly! In *The Billy-Goats Tough*, the Booing! Hissing! and 'corny' jokes are great fun to say aloud.

Remember to look at the audience and at the other actors, making sure that everyone can hear what you are saying.

Creating Sound Effects (FX)

You may like to add some sound effects throughout the play. Sounds to match the clopping of the Billy-Goats crossing the bridge, the rattling of toll money, and a superman-like *whoosh!* for Super Billy-Goat Tough's appearance, will all create extra atmosphere. See if there are any other places in the script where you could add sound effects.

Sets and Props

Once you have read the play, make a list of the things you will need. Here are some ideas to help your performance. You may like to add some of your own.

- Footbridge
- Tree stump
- Sign: Toll Bridge $3.75
- Backdrop of mountains
- Coins and money bag
- Copy of play script
- Glasses
- False teeth for Dracula
- Coloured bottle (HAIR-EX on label)
- Comb
- Oregano jar

Costumes

This play can be performed with or without costumes. If you wish to dress up, you may find the following useful.

- Cape and tights for Super Billy-Goat Tough (Superman-style 'S' on front)
- Black cape and pants for Dracula
- Suit for Advertiser
- Goat outfits: could be sheets with holes
- Hairy Troll costume: mop head for hair, brown hessian tunic

Have fun!

⋮ Ideas for guided reading ⋮

Learning objectives: prepare, read and perform playscripts: compare organisation of script with stories – how settings are indicated, storylines made clear; chart build up of play scene – how scenes start, how scenes are concluded; comment constructively on plays and performance, discussing effects and how they are achieved

Curriculum links: Citizenship: Choices

Interest words: Wonder Woman, Mr and Mrs Warlock, troll, Dracula, Blood Bank, Nyuk Nyuk

Resources: materials to make posters and invitations, whiteboard and pens

Casting: (1) Narrator **(2)** LBGT **(3)** SBGT **(4)** Borisina Dracula **(5)** Brian Troll **(6)** Advertiser **(All)** group and audience

Getting started

- Read the title and prompt children for the original title (*The Billy Goats Gruff*). Ask them to retell the original story from memory. How might this story be different?

- Read through p21 together to remind them of the key point in reading plays.

- Turn to p2. What do they think Super Billy Goats Tough (SBGT) and Little Billy Goats Tough (LBGT) will be like as characters? Discuss Borisina Dracula – what sort of person is she likely to be? Which story does she come from?

Reading and responding

- Encourage the children to read scene one aloud in role. Discuss their voices – are they convincing? Why/why not? Encourage them to guess what the next scene will bring.

- Read scene two together and praise use of phonic knowledge to read unfamiliar words.

- At the end of the scene, think back to the group's predictions about SBGT and LBGT. Were they right?

- Practise reading the rest of the play through in role. As a group, discuss what kind of play this is, which bits they think are most effective and why. Note them on a whiteboard.